Planet Protectors

HYDRO HERO

BookLife PUBLISHING

BookLife Publishing Ltd.
King's Lynn
Norfolk, PE30 4LS

Printed in Malaysia.

A catalogue record for this book is available from the British Library.

ISBN: 978-1-78637-653-4

Written by:
John Wood

Edited by:
Kirsty Holmes

Designed by:
Drue Rintoul

PHOTO CREDITS

All images are courtesy of Shutterstock.com. With thanks to Getty Images, Thinkstock Photo and iStockphoto. Front Cover – R-studio, Rich Carey. Throughout – Nadzin. 2 – DutchScenery. 4&5 – curiosity,. 6&7 – Paolo Bona, Dudarev Mikhail, Darkydoors. 8&9 – the8monkey, Rvector, fotobook. 10&11 – FreeBirdPhotos, mansong suttakarn. 12&13 – Tribalium, vicenfoto, Marnikus. 14&15 – Rich Carey, joyfull. 16&17 – S_Photo, Lorelyn Medina, Abscent. 18&19 – Rawpixel.com, a katz. 20&21 – Evgeniia Shelukhina, I-ing. 22&23 – ioat, Login.

CONTENTS

Words that look like **this** can be found in the glossary on page 24.

Time for a Mission

There are four Planet Protectors. We've looked after the environment since the beginning of time.

Look at Earth! Look at it! It's in trouble! Could you be the one to join our team, and save the world? Let's find out – we're going on a mission!

There will be questions throughout this book. Write down your answer to each one and check your score at the end!

Our base is called Trashy Island. It is a fortress made out of recycled stuff.

Ride the Wave

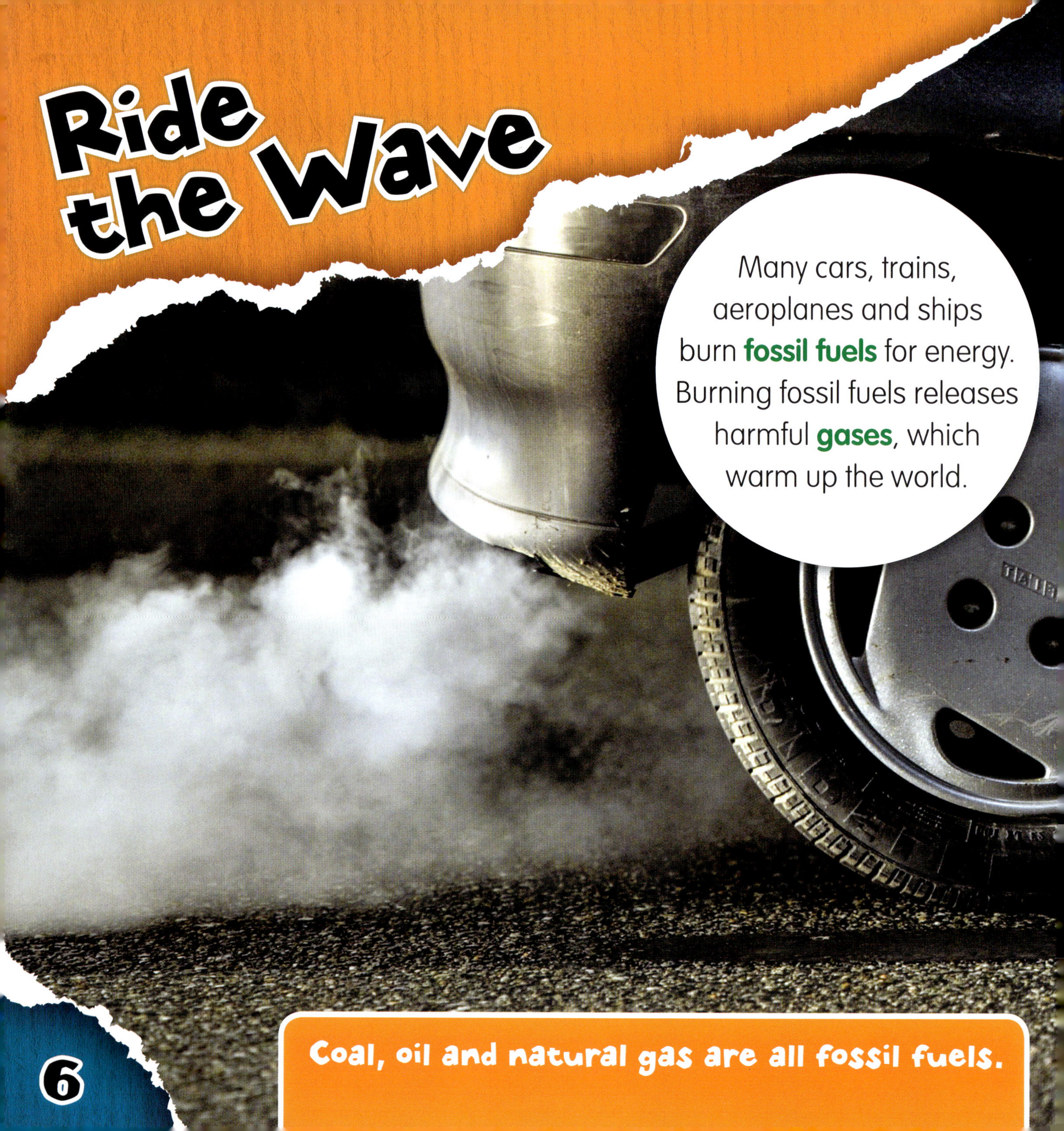

Many cars, trains, aeroplanes and ships burn **fossil fuels** for energy. Burning fossil fuels releases harmful **gases**, which warm up the world.

Coal, oil and natural gas are all fossil fuels.

When the temperature of Earth changes, it is called climate change. This is a big problem for many plants and animals all over the world.

These corals have turned white because of climate change, and they could soon die. This is called coral bleaching.

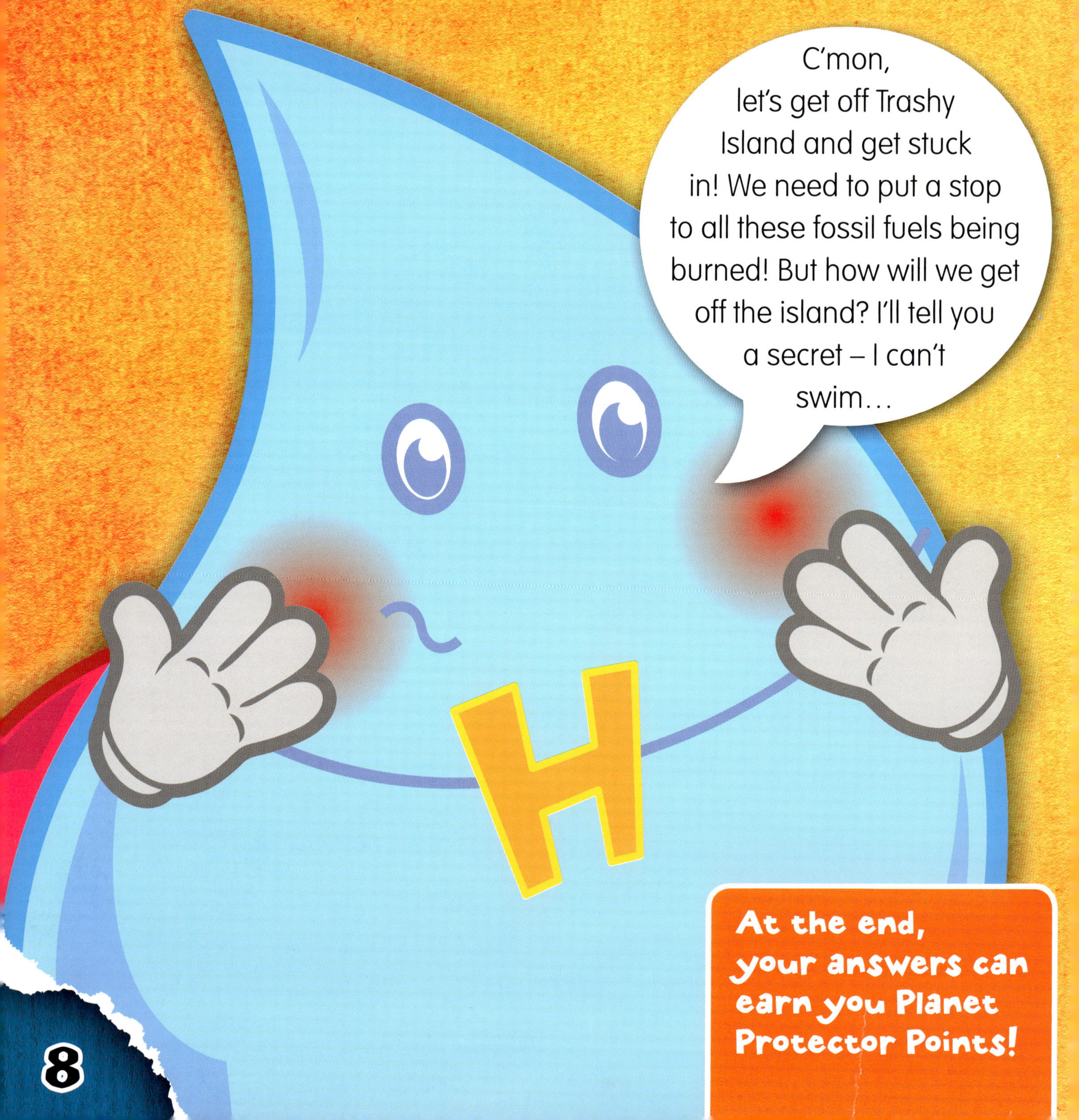

At the end, your answers can earn you Planet Protector Points!

Question 1

How will you travel from Trashy Island?

a) A ship powered by oil

b) A rowing boat big enough for two

c) We won't – let's stay on Trashy Island and forget about the world

Save the Water, Save the World

Most of the water on Earth is seawater, which humans cannot drink. This means we must look after the fresh water, so it is clean when it comes out of our taps.

It is important not to waste water.

The Earth recycles our drinking water, but it takes a long time. As long as we are careful with our water, it will never run out.

Heating up water uses a lot of electricity. This can also cause climate change.

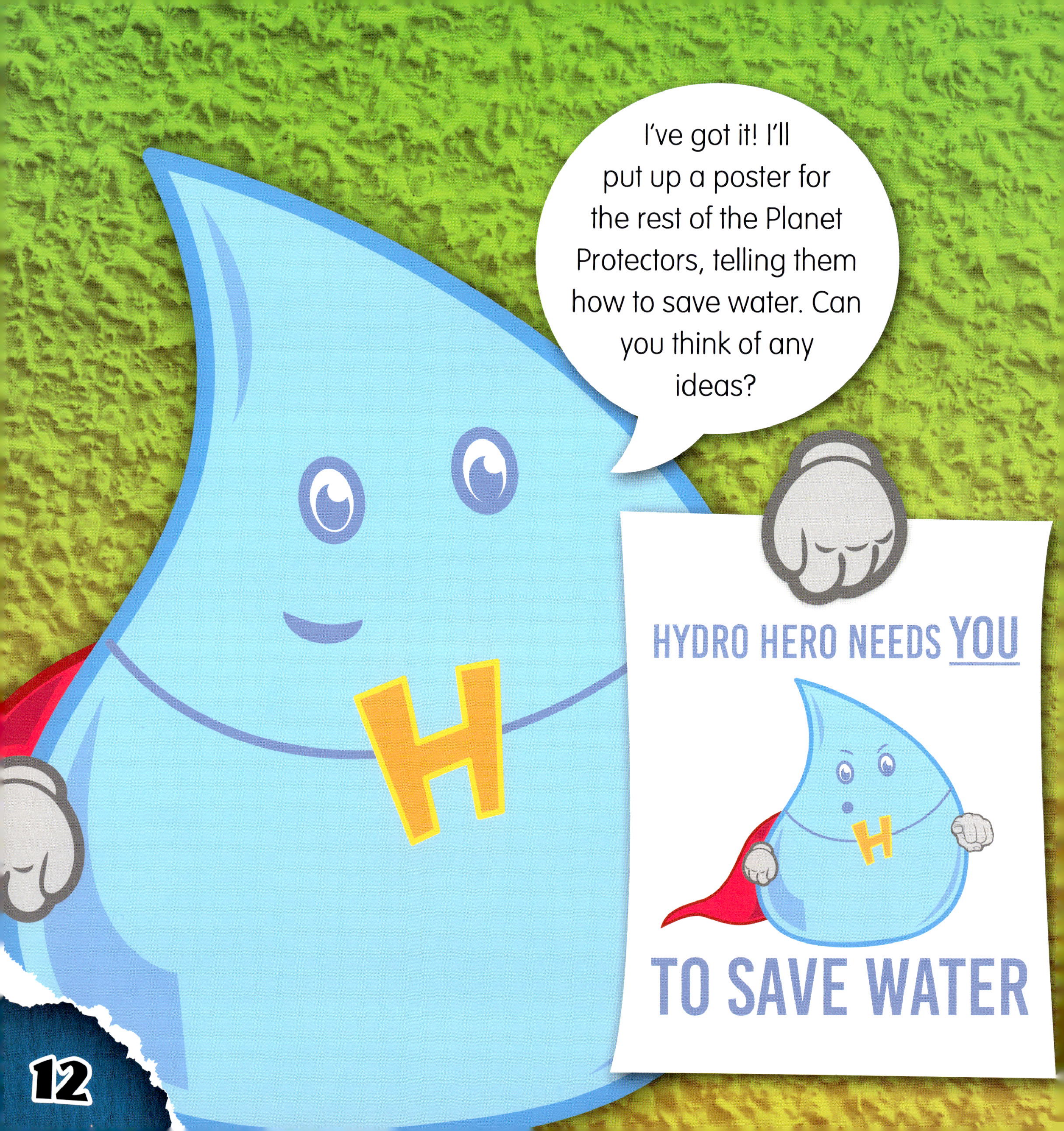
I've got it! I'll put up a poster for the rest of the Planet Protectors, telling them how to save water. Can you think of any ideas?
HYDRO HERO NEEDS YOU
H
TO SAVE WATER

Question 2

How can the Planet Protectors save water?

a) Turn off the tap while they brush their teeth

b) Stop drinking water completely

c) Have a shorter shower

Fight on the Beaches

A lot of our rubbish can end up in the ocean. Some rubbish, such as plastic, can be very harmful to animals and the environment.

Plastic may be eaten by fish and other animals. This can kill them.

Some people go on beach cleans. This means they walk up and down a beach picking up **litter** and making sure it gets safely recycled.

Beach cleans can stop rubbish being swept into the ocean.

Grab the litter-pickers! Get your gloves! Sound the alarm! We are going on a beach clean!

Question 3

How are you going to get people to join your beach clean?

a) Ask them once and give up if they say no

b) Say please over and over again until they agree

c) Tell them about all the animals they will save

Call in Help

It can be hard to make a big difference to the environment on your own. We must all work together to save the planet.

A government is a group of people that run a country. They make **laws** that can help or harm the environment.

It is important to talk to your government and tell them what we need for the planet.

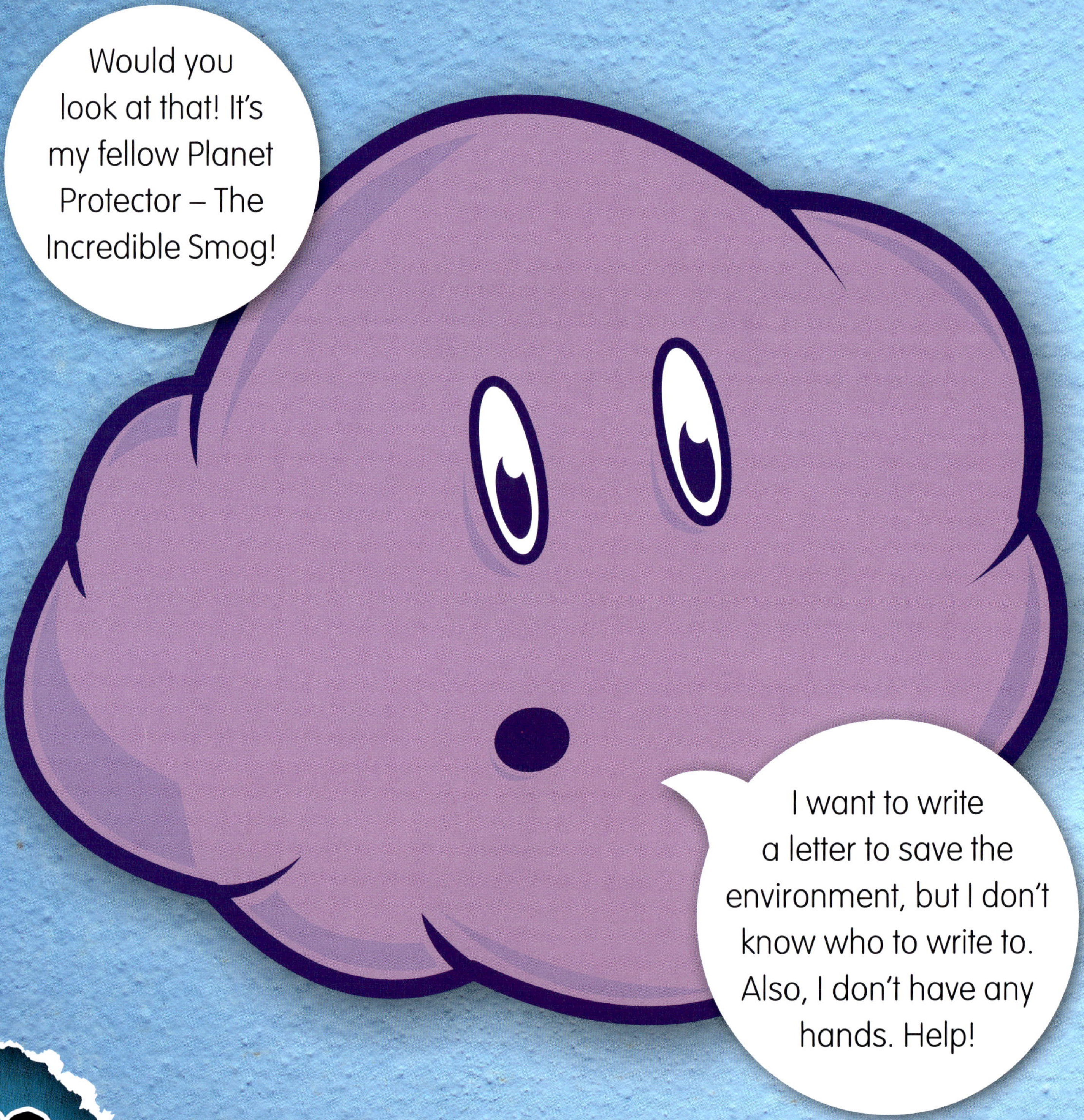
Would you look at that! It's my fellow Planet Protector – The Incredible Smog!
I want to write a letter to save the environment, but I don't know who to write to. Also, I don't have any hands. Help!

Question 4

Who should Smog write a letter to?

a) A member of the government, such as an MP

b) Your headteacher

c) Nobody – letters are for losers

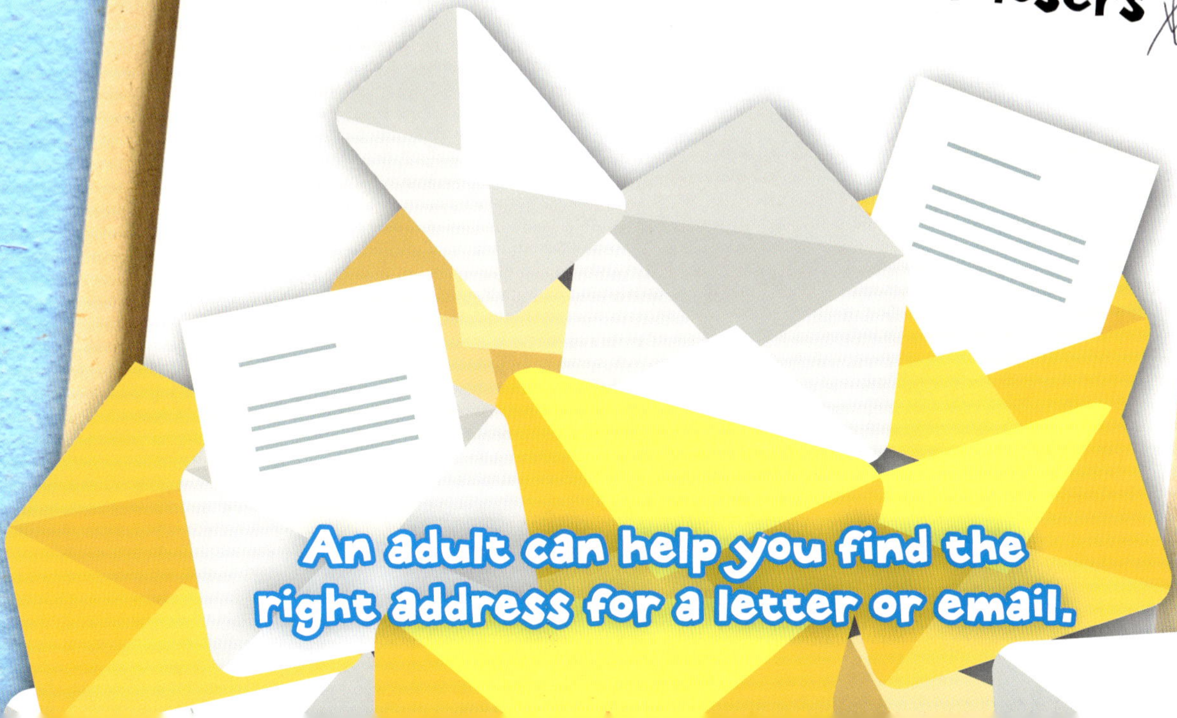

An adult can help you find the right address for a letter or email.

A New Planet Protector?

Question 1

A = 0 points

B = 2 points

C = 1 point

Question 2

A = 1 point

B = 0 points

C = 2 points

Question 3

A = 0 points

B = 1 point

C = 2 points

Question 4

A = 2 points

B = 1 point

C = 0 points

What did you get?

0-1

Oh no! You're an environmental disaster! Try again.

2-3

You've got a long way to go before you become a true Planet Protector.

4-5

You still have more to learn. Don't worry, you'll do better next time.

6-7

Not perfect, but you did very well. You would make a good side-kick.

8

Great score! You're our new Planet Protector! You start on Monday.

Glossary

electricity energy used to power machines and electronics

environment the natural world

fossil fuels fuels, such as coal, oil and gas, that formed millions of years ago from the remains of animals and plants

gases air-like substances that expand freely to fill any space available

laws rules that a country must follow

litter rubbish that has been dropped on the ground

MP member of parliament – a person chosen to speak for a certain area of the country

recycled used again to make something else

Index